D0990335

Hair ⭐ Magic

IMANI FINDS the RIGHT NOTES

written by Cicely Lewis

illustrated by Anastasia Magloire Williams

Lerner Publications ◆ Minneapolis

To my cousin Tasha. Thanks for braiding my hair every summer and keeping me cute!

Illustrations by Anastasia Magloire Williams

Lerner Publications Company
An imprint of Lerner Publishing Group, Inc.
241 First Avenue North
Minneapolis, MN 55401 USA

For reading levels and more information, look up this title at www.lernerbooks.com.

Main body text set in Mikado.
Typeface provided by HvD Fonts.

Image credits: Tom Copi/Getty Images, p. 39; Cicely Lewis portrait photo by Fernando Decillis.

Editor: Brianna Kaiser **Designer:** Emily Harris
Lerner team: Martha Kranes, Sue Marquis

Library of Congress Cataloging-in-Publication Data

Names: Lewis, Cicely, author. | Williams, Anastasia Magloire, illustrator.
Title: Imani finds the right notes / written by Cicely Lewis ; illustrated by Anastasia Magloire Williams.
Description: Minneapolis, MN : Lerner Publications Company, 2024. | Series: Hair magic (read woke chapter books), 02 | Audience: Ages 6–9. | Audience: Grades 2–3. | Summary: Imani is suffering from pre-recital nerves, but with the help of her magic hair she can regain her confidence and play the piano perfectly.
Identifiers: LCCN 2023005514 (print) | LCCN 2023005515 (ebook) | ISBN 9781728486895 (library binding) | ISBN 9798765615065 (epub)
Subjects: LCSH: African American girls—Juvenile fiction. | Piano—Performance—Juvenile fiction. | Self-confidence—Juvenile fiction. | Magic—Juvenile fiction. | CYAC: African Americans—Fiction. | Pianists—Fiction. | Self-confidence—Fiction. | Magic—Fiction. | BISAC: JUVENILE FICTION / Readers / Chapter Books | LCGFT: Readers (Publications)
Classification: LCC PZ7.1.L515 Imf 2024 (print) | LCC PZ7.1.L515 (ebook) | DDC 813.6 [Fic]—dc23/eng/20230207

LC record available at https://lccn.loc.gov/2023005514
LC ebook record available at https://lccn.loc.gov/2023005515

ISBN 979-8-7656-2422-7 (pbk.)

Manufactured in the United States of America
1-52812-50946-7/20/2023

TABLE OF CONTENTS

Imani's Hair Story

Hi! I'm Imani and I have a secret to tell you: my hair is magic.

It's true! Just ask my Grandma Dottie. All the women in my family have this special power. When I decide to make a change, I have magic inside of me to help. And then my hair magically changes!

4

Grandma Dottie

Mom

Auntie Neffie

Braids, beads, Afro puffs, twists, straight, or purple. There's no such thing as bad hair! I just need to say three magic words:

shimmer, sparkle, twirl.

Then poof! I have a new hairdo!

I hope you realize that you have special powers within you too. The next time you look in a mirror say, "I am beautiful because I am me." Because it's true!

Chapter 1
Starting Off-Key

Plink-a-plink-a-plink-a-plink . . . **PLUNK!**

Imani groaned as she hit the wrong note . . . again. The sound vibrated throughout the living room. Imani's weekly piano lesson with Ms. Ivy was not going well. Normally, she flew through her lessons with no problems.

But now she couldn't seem to play the right notes.

This is terrible, Imani thought with frustration. *I want to play beautifully like Nina Simone. The music recital is next week*!

Every time Imani thought about her upcoming performance, butterflies crowded her stomach. Her whole family was going to be there. She didn't want to mess up. She wanted them to see how well she played.

She imagined being on stage and the audience throwing tomatoes at her because her performance was so bad. She pictured Grandma Dottie crying because the music hurt her ears. She thought of her dad disguising himself in a coat and shades so no one could recognize he was her dad.

"Try again," Ms. Ivy said gently.

Imani nodded. She tried to erase all of these thoughts from her head and concentrate.

Plink-a-plink . . . **PLUNK!**

Her brother Isaiah peeped his head in the room. "You call that music?"

Imani glared at Isaiah until Ms. Ivy tapped the sheet music.

"You can do it," Ms. Ivy said. "You just need to relax and keep practicing. You have played this song before many times. It is normal to get the jitters before a big performance."

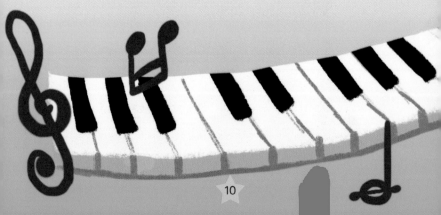

"Maybe I should play an easier song," Imani said.

Ms. Ivy raised an eyebrow. "I know you are up for the challenge. Don't let this off day discourage you."

"But I—"

"No buts," Ms. Ivy said as she pointed to the piano. "Let's try it again. From the top."

Imani's stomach sank. She sighed and continued to play.

All week long, Imani practiced in the morning before school. She practiced when she got home from school.

Sometimes she even practiced after dinner. But it seemed like the more she practiced, the worse she sounded.

She had a new dress and shoes for the recital. And Auntie Neffie had flat ironed her hair special for the recital. Everything was ready. But she still couldn't get the notes right.

PLUNK!

Chapter 2
Jumping In

Imani threw up her hands when she hit the wrong note . . . again. It was no use. The recital was tomorrow. Isaiah walked up to Imani and held up their dad's car keys.

"Isaiah, what do you want?" Imani asked.

"I am trying to help you find the right key!" he yelled. He fell on the floor, holding his stomach while laughing.

Imani rolled her eyes.

Their mom walked in and shot Isaiah a look. He immediately jumped up and ran away. She placed her hand on Imani's shoulder. "Imani, take a break and some deep breaths."

Imani took a deep breath but still felt nervous.

"Honey, I know you can do this," her mom said. "But you have to believe you can. You know, a lot of famous singers and musicians get nervous before they perform."

Really? Imani thought. *I'm sure Nina Simone never got nervous.*

"I know what will cheer you up." Her mom pointed to her watch. "Mallory's birthday party is starting soon. It will help take your mind off the recital."

Imani smiled a toothy grin. "I completely forgot! And it's at a water park!" Imani quickly grabbed her things and Mallory's gift.

When they arrived at the water park, Imani felt like a million bucks. Mallory and her mom waved from some poolside chairs.

"Happy birthday, Mal!" Imani said as they hugged.

"Thanks," Mallory said. "Let's go change."

"Don't forget this." Imani's mom waved her purple swimming cap. "I'm going to grab some lemonade. We'll meet by these chairs when you're not swimming."

Imani grabbed the cap from her mom and stuffed it in her bag. Then she and Mallory held hands as they walked to the changing rooms. They came out of their stalls at the same time.

Mallory squealed, "We're twins!" She pointed at Imani's suit, which was also green with orange polka dots.

After they dropped off their bags with Mallory's mom, Imani called out, "Last one in is a rotten egg!"

Imani reached the pool and **SPLASH!** Mallory jumped in right after her.

"I won!" Imani said. "You're a rotten egg!"

Mallory splashed water on Imani. "No, I'm not!"

Imani splashed back. Soon other kids from the party joined in and water splashed everywhere. Suddenly Mallory stopped splashing. "Imani, what's up with your hair?"

Imani raised her hands to her head. Her hair was no longer straight. "Oh no! I forgot my swimming cap!" She looked around the pool and spotted her mom. Her mom's eyes widened.

Chapter 3
Still Imani

Buzz, buzz.

The minute Imani's alarm woke her the morning after Mallory's party, it hit her. *No more straight hair for the recital today.*

Imani stretched her arms and sat up in bed. She had tossed and turned all night. She couldn't stop thinking about her performance and how her hair wouldn't look like she had planned for the recital.

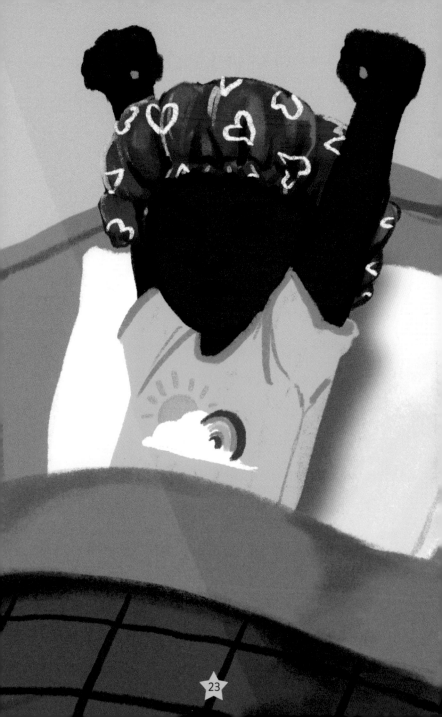

She got out of bed, took off her silk bonnet, and looked in her mirror above her dresser.

Woah!

Imani smiled at her hair. Her curly 'fro was truly a sight to behold. It looked like a halo around her head. She hadn't planned to wear her hair that way for the recital, but it was okay.

Imani's hair changed all the time. Sometimes she wore beads, sometimes she wore color extensions, sometimes she wore it straight. But no matter how she wore her hair, she was always the same person. "And every hairstyle looks beautiful," Imani whispered to herself.

And then she realized something else. "My hair may look different than I had planned, but I'm still the same girl who has been playing the piano for three years."

She grabbed her piano lesson book and looked at the notes and all the songs she had mastered. She remembered playing easier songs when she was first learning to play. Over time, she had moved on to harder songs.

The dates in her lesson book showed all the hours she had practiced.

I can do this, Imani thought. *I'm ready to play this song.*

"Shimmer, sparkle, twirl . . . I am a confident girl!"

Imani closed her eyes as a powerful, wonderful feeling washed over her. She felt tingles tickle her skin. When she opened her eyes, she beamed at the beautiful white flowers all over her Afro.

After she changed, Imani twirled into the living room wearing her new orange dress.

"Your hair is beautiful," Grandma Dottie said. "I love your Afro. Those flowers make you look like Billie Holiday. She always wore a flower in her hair when she sang."

Her mom hugged her. "You got this."

Imani smiled. "I do."

Imani and her family piled into the car. They listened to Nina Simone and Billie Holiday as her dad drove. Imani went through the notes in her head. Her fingers danced as she played her air piano.

Chapter 4
Performance Time

Imani was excited and ready as she waited backstage with the other performers. She flipped through her music book as she waited.

Her classmate Michael was standing next to her. He wouldn't stop biting his nails. "Are you okay?" Imani asked.

"Just a little nervous," he replied.

"Take a deep breath," Imani repeated the words her mom had told her. "You got this."

Michael breathed in and out. He grinned at her. "Thanks, Imani."

He walked onstage as they called his name. Imani closed her eyes and listened to Michael play the violin wonderfully.

Finally, it was her turn. She peeped out and saw her family sitting in the audience. They all were there to support her.

"Our next performer is Imani Tyson, and she will be playing the piano," Ms. Ivy announced. Imani took a deep breath. Michael gave her a thumbs-up as she walked onto the stage.

She sat down on the bench and placed her music on the piano. She flexed her fingers and then began to play.

Her music flowed throughout the concert hall. When she came to the part that she had messed up all week, her fingers danced across the keys in a beautiful rhythm.

Then she hit the last note.

The room erupted in applause. She heard her dad yell, "*Brava!*" Imani walked to the front of the stage and curtsied just like Ms. Ivy taught her.

After the recital was over, Imani's family gathered in the lobby for lemonade and cookies.

"Great job!" her dad exclaimed. He pulled a bouquet of flowers from behind his back. "It's tradition to give flowers after a great performance. But it looks like someone beat me to it." He winked as he looked at the flowers in her hair.

Imani smiled. "Thanks Dad! These are beautiful. I worked hard. I just needed to believe in myself and go for it."

Grandma Dottie handed her a cookie. "Attagirl!"

"Little man, what did you think of your big sister's performance?" their mom asked Isaiah. He had two cookies, one in each hand, and was chewing more cookies.

He mumbled through a mouth full of crumbs, "It didn't sound like the song you played at home."

Imani put her free hand on her hip. "That's because I found the right key this time." Everyone, including Isaiah, laughed along with her joke.

THINK ABOUT IT

⭐ Imani was inspired by Nina Simone. Who inspires you?

⭐ Tell about a time when things didn't go the way you planned. What did you learn from it?

⭐ How can you help someone when they are nervous or scared?

MUSICAL SIMONE

Nina Simone was a gifted singer, songwriter, and pianist who told stories through her music. She was born Eunice Kathleen Wayman. By age three, she started playing piano by ear. That meant she could play music she heard without looking at sheet music. When she was twenty-four years old, she signed with a record label. She started making albums and her music reached a wider audience.

Simone made dozens of albums during her career. Her music blended pop, jazz, folk, and rhythm and blues. She was often called the "High Priestess of Soul" because she played so beautifully that audiences would lose track of time while they listened to her perform. She died on April 1, 2003. But she left behind a huge legacy.

ABOUT THE AUTHOR

As a young girl, Cicely Lewis loved combing her doll's hair and doodling different hairstyles in the margins of her notebook. She didn't always see images that looked like her in books and television. This is one of the reasons she started the Read Woke challenge when she grew up. As a school librarian, she encourages her students to take action in their community and to love themselves. She promotes books that celebrate what makes people special and original.

ABOUT THE ILLUSTRATOR

Anastasia Magloire Williams is an illustrator, storyteller, and graphic designer living in sunny Florida. It is her passion to paint colorful adventures, reveal important history, and tell untold stories that reflect the diverse world we all share. Just like in the book *Wild, Wild Hair*, she had a complicated relationship with her big Afro as a child. But with the help of her amazing stylist Okeya, she has learned to love her magical hair!